PUFFIN BOOKS

Happy Christmas, Rita!

Happy Christmas, Rita!

Written and illustrated by
Hilda Offen

PUFFIN BOOKS

For Lucy and Sally Gill

PUFFIN BOOKS

Published by the Penguin Group
Penguin Books Ltd, 27 Wrights Lane, London W8 5TZ, England
Penguin Books USA Inc., 375 Hudson Street, New York, New York 10014, USA
Penguin Books Australia Ltd, Ringwood, Victoria, Australia
Penguin Books Canada Ltd, 10 Alcorn Avenue, Toronto, Ontario, Canada M4V 3B2
Penguin Books (NZ) Ltd, 182–190 Wairau Road, Auckland 10, New Zealand

Penguin Books Ltd, Registered Offices: Harmondsworth, Middlesex, England

First published by Hamish Hamilton Ltd 1993
Published in Puffin Books 1996
1 3 5 7 9 10 8 6 4 2

Copyright © Hilda Offen, 1993
All rights reserved

The moral right of the author/illustrator has been asserted

Filmset in Plantin

Made and printed by Imago Ltd, Hong Kong

It was the day before Christmas.

"It's snowing!" said Rita.

"Hurray!" cried Julie. "I'll go skating!"

"And we can take the sledge out!" said Jim and Eddie.

"You'll all have to wait until the snow stops!" said Mrs Potter.

In the afternoon the sun came out and the Potter children ran to put on their outdoor clothes.

"Where's my coat?" asked Rita. "And my wellingtons? I left them in a bag by the door."

"A yellow plastic bag?" asked Eddie.
"Oops! Sorry, Rita! I thought they were
jumble. I gave them to the lady from the
Dogs' Home."

"You'll have to stay in, Rita!" called Mrs
Potter. "You can't go out without your
warm clothes."

Rita watched as the children raced away.
She felt really sad. Then she had an idea.

"My Rescuer's outfit!" she said.

She raced upstairs and took the box from
under her bed.

8

She put on her tights, her tunic and her cloak. She put on her yellow gloves and her belt. And last of all she put on her boots with wings on the heels. Rita Potter had disappeared! In her place stood – Rita the Rescuer!

"Here we go!" cried Rita and she zoomed out of the window. She felt as warm as toast!

As Rita flew up the street she
spotted little Robbie Russell.
He was looking at a snowflake
through his magnifying glass.

"Look out, Robbie!" shouted
the people round about.

A giant icicle had fallen from
the roof above him!

"He's had it!" gasped
the crowd.

"Not while I'm here!" cried Rita, and she puffed as hard as she could. Her hot breath melted the icicle and turned it into a shower of rain. Little Robbie was soaked.

"Never mind!" said Rita, and she huffed and puffed him dry again.

Suddenly a scream rang out.

"Got to go!" cried Rita.

"I recognise that voice."

Jim and Eddie's sledge had taken a
wrong turn. It was heading for the quarry!
"Help!" screamed Jim and Eddie.

Rita cut through the cold air like a knife. She pulled the sledge to a halt on the edge of a sheer drop.

"It's the Rescuer again!" gasped Eddie.

Rita dragged them back up the hill and pushed them down the safe slope.

"Be more careful in future!" she called.

At the bottom of the hill Mrs Simpkins was digging like mad.

"I've lost my dog, Tiger!" she cried. "I think he's buried somewhere in this snow-drift."

"I'll find him for you," said Rita. "I have X-ray eyes."

She took the shovel from Mrs Simpkins
and snow flew everywhere as she dug
deeper and deeper into the drift. In no time
at all she had lifted Tiger out of the snow.

"Thank you, thank you!" cried Mrs Simpkins; but Rita couldn't stay to chat. She had heard more screams and a loud cracking sound!

Julie and her best friend Tania were skating on the pond. Oh no! The ice was beginning to crack.

"They'll be drowned!" cried the people on the bank.

"No they won't!" said Rita. She grabbed
Julie and Tania just as the ice gave way
beneath them. Then she flew them back to
the edge of the pond.

"Thanks, Rescuer!" said Julie. "Can we
have your autograph?"

But Rita wasn't listening. A low rumbling
filled the air. It got louder and louder and
louder.

A giant snowball was rolling towards the
town. It rumbled on, getting bigger and
bigger all the time.

"Help!" cried the people. "The town will
be destroyed!"

Rita moved with the speed of light.
Pow! She hit the snowball as hard as
she could. It burst into a million trillion
pieces and fell like snow on to the
roof-tops beneath.

"Hurray!" cheered the crowd. "The
Rescuer's saved our town!"

No one could thank Rita enough. They
built a huge snow Rescuer in the Market
Place and Rita helped them with the
difficult bits.

"It will stay there until the snow melts," said the mayor, "to remind us of the day you saved us, Rescuer!"

"I'm glad I could help!" said Rita.

It was beginning to get dark, so Rita started off for home. On the way she passed Basher Briggs, who was snowballing some toddlers.

"Let's see how *you* like it!" said Rita, and she threw a hundred snowballs at Basher, all within the space of a second.

"Stop!" yelled Basher. "I'll never do it again – I promise!"

"Well – that was a good day's work!"
thought Rita as she sped through the starry
sky. "Hallo! What's that?"

Two boots were sticking out of a chimney
pot. Some reindeer stamped their hooves
nearby.

Rita swooped down. She grasped the boots and pulled as hard as she could. "One – two – three – heave!" she cried.

There was a Pop! and a shower of soot – and out shot Father Christmas!

"I must have had one mince-pie too many!" he said. "I'm sure I got down that chimney last year. Thank you, Rescuer!"

"It was a pleasure!" said Rita. "Happy Christmas, Father Christmas!"

"The same to you!" he said.

Rita flew back home and changed into
her ordinary clothes. Then she went
downstairs.

Eddie, Julie and Jim were decorating the
Christmas tree.

"What a shame you had to stay indoors,
Rita!" said Jim. "You missed the Rescuer
again!"

"She stopped our sledge from falling into
the quarry!" said Eddie.

"She grabbed me and Tania just as we
were about to go through the ice!" said
Julie.

"She saved the town from being flattened by a giant snowball!" cried Jim.

"Well, I never!" said Rita.

On Christmas morning Rita woke early. At the end of her bed was a gigantic stocking – the biggest one she had ever seen!

It was bursting with toys and books and sweets. There was even a new coat and a pair of boots.

"Happy Christmas, everyone!" cried Rita.

Also available in First Young Puffin

DUMPLING
Dick King-Smith

Dumpling wishes she could be long and sausage-shaped like other dachshunds. When a witch's cat grants her wish Dumpling becomes the longest dog ever.

BUBBLEGUM BOTHER
Wendy Smith

Bobby is a real bubblegum lover. In fact he is known as Bubbles, the Champion Balloon Blower. One day his friend, Blue, gives him a tasty new kind of gum to try. But Bobby doesn't look at the instructions on the wrapper . . . and goes on to blow the most unusual, magical balloon ever!

BELLA AT THE BALLET
Brian Ball

Bella has been looking forward to her first ballet lesson for ages – but she's cross when Mum says Baby Tommy is coming with them. Bella is sure Tommy will spoil everything, but in the end it's hard to know who enjoys the class more – Bella or Tommy!